Paddington Bear

Goes to the Hospital

MICHAEL BOND and KAREN JANKEL
Pictures by R. W. ALLEY

HarperCollins*Publishers*

Paddington Bear Goes to the Hospital.
Text copyright © 2001 by Michael Bond and Karen Jankel. Illustrations copyright © 2001 by R.W. Alley. First Published in Great Britain by Collins in 2001. Collins
is an imprint of HarperCollins Publishers Ltd. First American Edition 2001. Printed in Singapore. All rights reserved. Library of Congress card number 00-109012
www.harperchildrens.com

Paddington lay back on the lawn with his paws in the air and gazed up at the Browns. "Where am I?" he gasped.

"You're at home, dear," said Mrs. Brown. "At number thirty-two, Windsor Gardens."

"Is that in Darkest Peru?" asked Paddington.

"If you ask me," said Mrs. Bird, "that bear's lost his memory."

"Oh dear, Henry!" exclaimed Mrs. Brown. "What shall we do?"

Mr. Brown consulted his medical dictionary. "All it says here is 'the victim shouldn't drive a car.'"

"I don't think I could anyway," said Paddington. "I've hurt my shoulder."

"Would you like a bun?" suggested Mrs. Brown.

"What's a bun?" asked Paddington.

"That settles it," said Mrs. Bird.

"I'm calling the hospital!"

"I'm sorry we took so long," said the ambulance driver. "When I heard the name 'Paddington' I went to the railway station by mistake.

"If you ask me," he said, "this young bear's not only lost his memory, he's hurt his shoulder, as well. One of you ladies had better come with him in case he has to stay in the hospital overnight."

"Thank goodness I put his clean pajamas out this morning," said Mrs. Bird, trying to strike a cheerful note.

The ambulance crew soon made up for lost time, and with sirens wailing, Paddington reached the hospital in no time at all.

"Stand by for a young bear emergency," said the driver to the waiting staff, and with a count of three, they lifted Paddington on to a bed.

"Is it true that you've lost your memory?" asked a doctor.

"Would you mind repeating the question?" replied Paddington. "*Phew! Phew!*"

"I don't like the sound of his wheezes," said a nurse.

"I think we've got complications," agreed the doctor. "He'd better go straight to X ray."

"You've got complications!" exclaimed Paddington indignantly. "What about me? *Phew! Phew!*"

Paddington had never traveled anywhere on a bed before, and he thought it was very good value. "There was nothing like this in Darkest Peru," he announced as they gathered speed.

"*Phew! Phew!*"

When they reached the X-ray room, the lady in charge pushed
a large machine over the bed and made some adjustments.

"Now lie very still while I take some pictures," she said.
"Otherwise, they will come out blurred."

With that she went to the other side of the room, pressed a
button, and there was a whirring noise.

"Cheese!" said Paddington.

Afterward, Paddington and Mrs. Brown met the doctor again.

Paddington stared at the pictures on the wall. "What's happened to my fur?" he exclaimed. "I had it when I came in."

"It's still there," said the doctor. "This is a special camera for looking inside people—and bears, too," he added hastily.

"It looks very complicated," said Paddington. "I didn't know I had so much inside me."

"The one on the left shows why your shoulder's hurting," explained the doctor. "The bone's come out of its socket. We will need to put you to sleep while we relocate it."

"Have you had anything to eat since breakfast?" asked a nurse.

"I haven't even had time for my elevenses," said Paddington.

"That's good," said the nurse, wiping his arm with something cold. "Otherwise you would have had to wait while it settled."

Paddington felt a tiny prick, and he was about to give the nurse a hard stare . . .

. . . when his eyelids began to droop.

As soon as he was asleep the doctor turned to Mrs. Brown. "We'll soon put things right. He won't feel a thing.

"As for his memory, it probably needs a jog, but a good night's rest often works wonders. I must say I'm a bit worried about his breathing, though."

"It's a mystery," said Mrs. Brown. "He's never had this problem before."

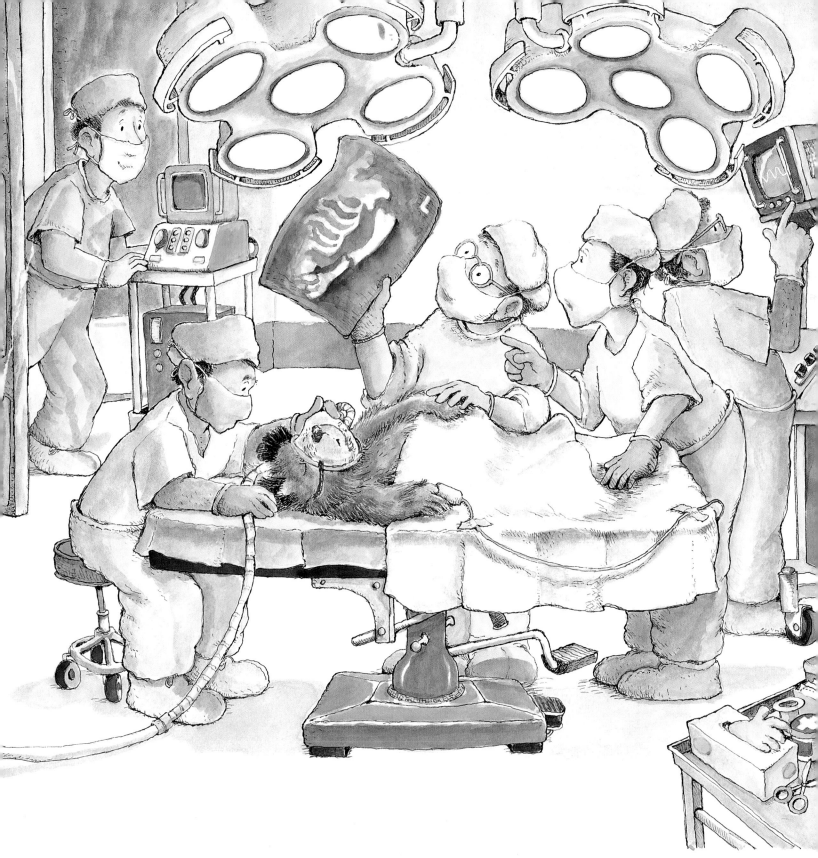

Paddington woke to find himself in a strange room.

"Where am I?" he asked for the second time that day.

"You're in a ward with lots of other patients," said Mrs. Brown. "And the doctor's put your arm back in its socket."

"I hope it's pointing the right way," said Paddington. "Otherwise, I won't know whether I'm coming or going."

"I've brought you some water," said a nurse. "I expect you're feeling thirsty after your operation."

"I am," said Paddington.

He was about to ask for something more exciting to drink, but he couldn't think of the name.

"Tea?" suggested Mrs. Brown.

"Bless you!" said Paddington.

"I expect they will keep you in overnight for observation," said Mrs. Brown.

"I don't think I want anyone observing me asleep," said Paddington. "I might fall out of bed."

"Don't worry," said the nurse. "The sides lift up to stop that from happening."

"Besides, I won't be far away," said Mrs. Brown.

At that moment Mr. Brown arrived, carrying a bowl of fruit from all the traders in the market and a get-well-soon card from Paddington's friend, Mr. Gruber.

"Even Mr. Curry sent his best wishes," he said. "How nice it is to be popular!"

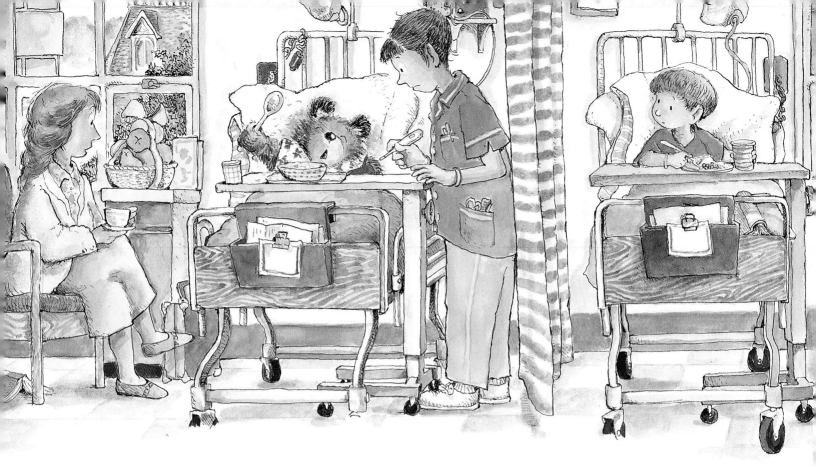

Later an orderly appeared with some food. "Oh dear," she said. "Don't tell me the boy who was in this bed has gone home. He always liked his food hot and spicy."

"Don't worry," said Paddington eagerly. "I'll have it."

"There's nothing wrong with that bear's appetite," said a nurse, eyeing the empty plate.

"There is now!" gasped Paddington. And this time his "*phews!*"
sounded as though he really meant them, since he had never
before tasted anything quite so hot.

"I think I'd better save taking your temperature until you've
cooled down," said the nurse. "I'll simply feel your pulse and be
getting on with it."

Just then two more nurses came along, pushing a cart laden with bottles and jars.

"It's medicine time," said one of them, handing Paddington a small cup filled with pink liquid.

"I'd like another one of those, please," he announced.

"I think it's making me better already."

The nurse laughed. "I wish we had more patients like you."

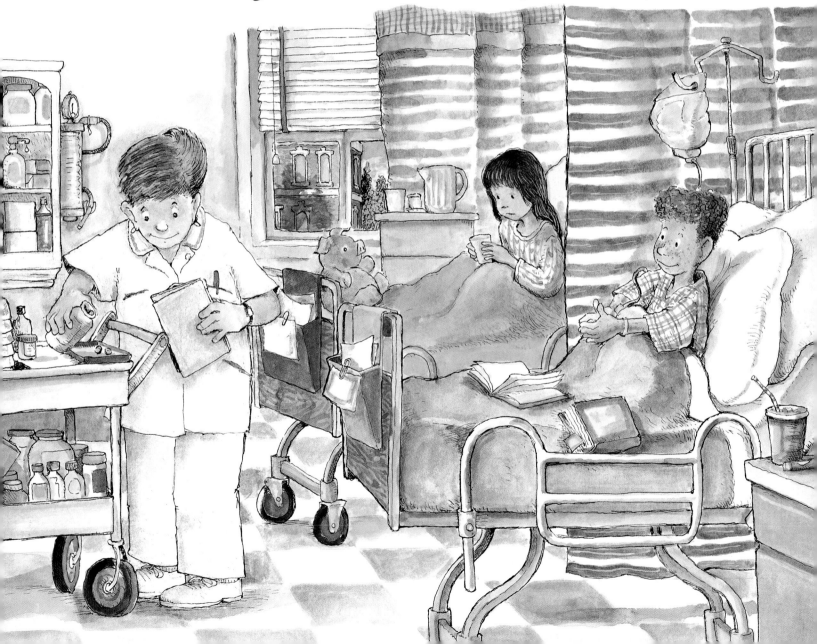

When it was bedtime, Mrs. Brown helped Paddington wash his whiskers and clean his teeth.

"If you need anything during the night," she said, "just press the emergency button and someone will come."

"Sleep tight," she said, lifting the sides on the bed.

"Oh, I will," murmured Paddington. So much had happened to him he felt as though he might sleep forever.

"I think," he announced to the world in general, "I might have an emergency button by my bed when I get home. Sometimes I want things during the night."

But he didn't have time to test the one in the hospital, for he was soon fast asleep.

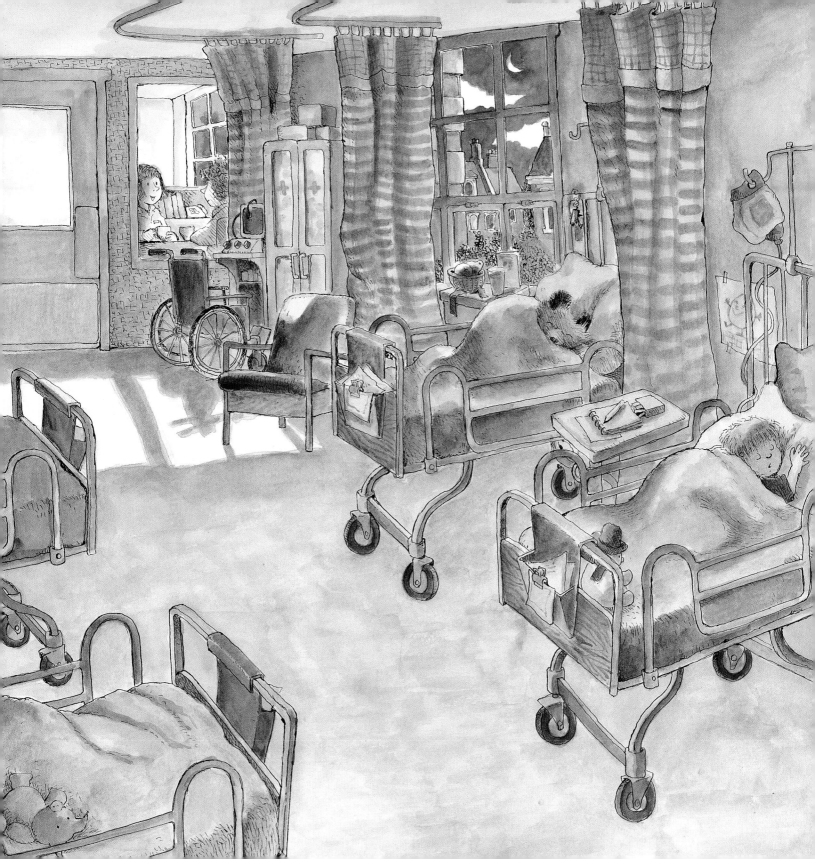

The next morning Paddington
went for a walk around the ward to
meet the other patients.

One small boy had just had his
tonsils removed.

Another had fallen out
of a tree and broken his leg.

A girl had been rushed in to
have her appendix out.

And another boy had been hit by a car when he ran across the road without looking.

Paddington decided he was really very lucky.

"You can always see people worse off than yourself in a hospital," said a nurse.

"I can see why they're called patients," said Paddington. "Some of them must have to wait a very long time before they get better."

To Paddington's surprise, when he got back
to his bed he found he had visitors.

Mr. Brown held up an L-shaped piece of wood. "Do you recognize this?" he asked. "I found it when I was cutting the grass this morning."

"It's my boomerang!" exclaimed Paddington. "The one you gave me for my birthday. It's all coming back to me."

"Like it did yesterday morning!" said Mrs. Bird. "Blessed thing! It must have flown back when you were testing it and hit you on the head."

"That's the trouble with boomerangs," said Jonathan. "They always come back."

"You'd better duck next time," agreed Judy.

"It's all your fault, Henry," said Mrs. Brown. "No wonder Paddington lost his memory."

"Well, at least it seems to have been jogged back again," said Mr. Brown defensively.

"Phew! Phew!" agreed Paddington.

"And that's another thing," said Mrs. Bird. She held up a small silver object. "Guess what?"

"It's the present you gave me in case I ever have an emergency," said Paddington. "It must have fallen out of my pocket."

He held the object up to his mouth and blew—"*Phew, phew!*"

Several piercing blasts brought doctors and nurses running from all directions.

"It's nice to know it isn't broken. When I lost my memory, I forgot I needed a whistle to make my *phews* work," said Paddington.

"All's well that ends well," said the doctor, as the Browns explained what had happened.

"It's been a learning experience for us, too," he added, amid general agreement.

"It could be very useful if we have any more bear patients to look after."

"I'm glad you had me to practice on," said Paddington, as he waved good-bye. "I've never been in a hospital before, and now that I know what goes on, I won't mind coming back!"